Spaceports & Spidersilk

February 2021

Edited by Marcie Lynn Tentchoff

Spaceports & Spidersilk
February 2021
Edited by Marcie Lynn Tentchoff

Story and art copyrights owned by the respective authors and artists
Cover art "Conjuring the Dragon" by Richard H. Fay
Cover design by Laura Givens

First Printing, February 2021

Hiraeth Publishing
P.O. Box 1248
Tularosa, NM 88352
e-mail: sdpshowcase@yahoo.com

Visit www.hiraethsffh.com for science fiction, fantasy, horror, scifaiku, and more. While you are there, visit the Shop for books and more! **Support the small, independent press...**

Stories

Poetry

Illustrations

From the Editor...

Conflict. As a concept the word is not entirely pleasant. It can refer to disagreement or to war, to mildly embarrassing situations or to deadly peril, to a too-difficult exam paper or to a world-saving riddle. Very few people (other than internet trolls) enjoy dealing with conflict,

But writers are very odd people.

From a writer's point of view, conflict is not only positive, it is essential. Without conflict, stories become insipid and boring. What is a hero without a reason to behave heroically? What is a villain without someone or something to confront? If a tale is made up of simple, un-conflicted existence, with no reason to struggle, or learn or grow, why would anyone read it? No, to make for a good story, an exciting, riveting, edge-of-your-seat story, things have to go wrong, life has to get difficult, and the protagonists have to work for their (we hope) happy ending.

Luckily, the stories and poems within this, the February 2021 issue of Spaceports & Spidersilk, each hold plenty of conflict. The protagonists you find here will be confronted with mysterious hauntings, perilous math problems, devious creatures, and dangerous settings and situations.

It is how they deal with those conflicts that weaves the hearts of the stories, and draws us, as readers, into their adventure-filled worlds.

Happy reading!
Marcie Lynn Tentchoff

Pyra and the Tektites
By Tyree Campbell

Pyra and the Tektites

Pyra, age thirteen, is running away from home in the Asteroid Belt because she's not doing well in school. Her parents want to send her to Mars for school, and she doesn't want to go. She sneaks aboard a cargo shuttle, and falls asleep in the hold. When she awakens, she finds herself in free-fall; the shuttle has been seized by the Tektites, a group of rebel pirates . . .

. . . and the adventures begin!

This volume encompasses the first three novellas:
Aquarium in Space
The Unicorn Stone
Smugglers!

Order a copy here:
https://www.hiraethsffh.com/product-page/pyra-and-the-tektites-by-tyree-campbell

The Wight of the Well

Lawrence Buentello

Solomon first heard the voice coming from the well the morning his father sent him off with three buckets to fill.

That he was only a young boy, and carrying three full buckets of well water was going to prove a significant challenge for his small, thin body, seemed not to matter to his father, nor to his mother, who simply scoffed at his complaints. She told him that if he wanted her to make him any bread to eat then he would take up the buckets and fulfill his parents' wishes. His older brother, Thomas, who was as hard a worker as any young man of the village, often laughed that Solomon was the laziest boy in all the provinces. Solomon doubted his brother could know this, for who would ever conduct such a survey? There had to be at least *one* lazier boy than him.

Admonished, Solomon took up his buckets, and, since he was fairly hungry, walked from the little thatched house in the glade to the distant well which his family shared with two other families in that wilderness.

A long length of rope lay coiled by the

rock ring encircling the mouth of the well, and, after sliding away the wooden cover that kept leaves and all manner of crawling things from falling in, it was to this rope that he tied the first bucket before lowering it into the shadows of the pit. A stake held the rope firmly to the ground, so there was no danger of losing it should his grip falter, but still Solomon exhibited great care in dropping the bucket into the water, carefully listening for a splash from the depths, before drawing it up again, hand over hand, being careful to keep as much of the contents from spilling as possible.

He repeated this process two more times, setting the full buckets next to one another, before sliding the wooden cover back over the mouth of the well and coiling the rope again for one of the other families to use.

He was calculating, as young boys without much practical experience do, the way in which he might carry all three buckets at once—without spilling significant water, which would bring him only grief should he arrive back home with half-filled buckets—when he heard a voice, small but distinct, echoing faintly from the well.

Could someone have possibly fallen in? But how could they have fallen with the wooden cover in place?

Solomon stepped to the stone ring and fell to his knees, listening. Perhaps he'd mistaken the distant cry of birds for a voice

—but, no, he *did* hear a voice calling from the well, he wasn't mistaken. So the boy pulled away the protective cover from the stone ring and called down.

"Hello? Is anyone down there?"

"Yes, I am down in the well," a small voice echoed up, which seemed to belong to a young girl.

Now Solomon grew excited, for the opportunity seemed to have arrived for him to be a hero, like all the heroes of the tales of knights and gentry he was fond of hearing. His father did not often recite such stories, since he was a plain, sober man, but when he did the boy always listened with rapt attention. Noble men rescuing damsels! Knights on horses in battle with winged beasts!

"You've fallen into the water!" Solomon said, reaching for the coil of rope. "I'll lower down the rope to you. Can you climb up? I'm not sure I can pull you up by myself, but I can always run for my brother—"

"No," the voice said, "I haven't fallen into the well. I *live* in the well!"

Now the boy's excitement turned to bewilderment, for he didn't understand how anyone, let alone a young girl by the sound of the voice, could actually live in a deep pit full of water. But he was certain the voice rose up from the depths—what could she possibly mean?

"I don't understand. How can you live in a

well?"

"If I may say, I live *well* in the well." The voice laughed childishly, causing Solomon to smile, too, though uncertainly.

"I've never known of anyone who could live down a well. Most everyone would drown! Are you sure you're not drowning?"

"I'm very sure. I couldn't be living if I were drowning."

Well, that much made sense to the boy, but not much else. "What is your name? Do you belong to one of the families in the village?"

"I am Brixa, and belong to no family. What is your name?"

"Solomon. My father is a farmer, and we use this well."

"I spied your face as you leaned over. You are young, Solomon, and still able to hear me. Those who are older and disbelieving of magical things quickly lose the ability to hear someone like me. I'm glad you can hear me!"

Solomon didn't know what to think of this declaration, so instead he asked, "How is it that you came to live down our well?"

As the boy listened, kneeling before the dark mouth of the abyss, the voice of Brixa spun a wondrous tale of magic spirits born into the natural world: some were born to live amongst the trees, cavorting among the branches and seen as will-o-the-wisps to ordinary people, some were born to live in the mountains and mine deep into the earth

11

in search of gold and jewels, and some were born to live in the lakes and rivers, flashing beneath the waves and beguiling those within their sailing vessels and boats.

But all lived in a world that was half-nature and half-magic, so that they also lived in ethereal palaces and cottages no one but the enchanted could inhabit. Brixa had lived in the river for many years, happily moving through the waters until she followed the path of the river into an underground spring, and became lost in the dark watercourses beneath the land. Finally, her travels ceased when she arrived in a great underground reservoir, the same reservoir providing fresh water to the well below the boy.

In this reservoir, Brixa constructed a magical palace built of enchanted marble, alabaster, and lapis lazuli, and filled its rooms with instruments and treasures from the spirit world; beautiful music filled the spaces of the rooms, and wonderful aromas permeated the waters.

But she lived alone in her palace, and was so very lonely.

"Solomon," the voice said, full of joy, "climb down into the well and I will show you my palace and everything it holds. Please, join me!"

"I couldn't," Solomon said, rising to his feet. "My father said that if I climbed down into the well, I would die. I would drown, Brixa, because I'm not magical. I'm sorry."

"But I'll protect you. My magic will keep you safe, Solomon. Climb down the rope and join me in my palace!"

For a moment the boy leaned over the ring of stones and stared down into the deep dark shaft, wondering if Brixa's words were true. But then he shook his head, remembering his father's stern warning. Now he realized how long he'd tarried at the well without bringing back the buckets, and he knew he had to leave for home or face punishment for his tardiness.

"I'll come back tomorrow to talk to you," he said, sliding the wooden cover back over the mouth of the well. "I promise."

"Don't leave!" the voice called up, muffled by the covering. "Please, Solomon!"

The boy gathered the heavy buckets and, spilling more than a little of the water they contained because he was still thinking of Brixa and her magical palace within the well, managed to carry all the buckets back to the house without tripping over his own feet.

***

That evening, as Solomon and his family sat before a small evening meal, he said, as he prepared to take a bite from his portion of bread, "Today I talked to a spirit that lives at the bottom of the well."

Solomon's father, mother, and brother sat in disbelief, his words having the same effect as if he'd used profane language. His mother and father glanced at one another, while his

13

brother merely shook his head.

"What is this about?" his father asked.

With great enthusiasm, for he believed there was nothing wrong with telling the truth, he recounted his trip to the well, as they might remember having sent him off with three buckets to fill, which were indeed heavy on the return, and the wondrous conversation he had with the spirit, Brixa. As his family watched him with wide eyes, he spoke at length of the dimensions of her palace, and of the treasures she assured him awaited his arrival within the well. When he was finished speaking, he filled his mouth with the last of his bread and wondered if he might have another portion.

His mother frowned at his father, her lovely face crossed with concern—Solomon had seen this expression before on less than happy occasions. "I told you that it was foolish to fill his head with fables of dragons and monsters. Now he's making up stories of his own."

Solomon swallowed hurriedly and said, "It's not a story. All that I told you really happened."

His father's bushy eyebrows fell upon his eyes wearily. "Solomon, there is no such a thing as a spirit living at the bottom of a well."

"I swear, it's true! She invited me down into the well to see her palace!"

"You know I told you to never climb down

into that well. It's dangerous. And you might not have the strength to climb back up."

"He's lying," Thomas said, laughing. "He's making up a story to get out of work."

"That's not true," Solomon said, perplexed by his family's disbelief. "Why would I say such a thing to get out of work?"

"Why would he?" his fathered asked his elder son.

"It's simple," Thomas replied. "He tells you a story about being invited to climb down into the well." Here he pointed dramatically toward Solomon. "You become afraid the little dunce will actually fall into the well and break his neck, so you never send him to fetch water again."

"Don't call your brother names," their mother admonished.

But she and Solomon's father again exchanged glances, which meant, at least to Solomon, who was used to their looks when it came to his disposition, that they believed Thomas more than him. This seemed an unfair circumstance, since he was only telling the truth.

"Solomon," his father said sternly, "I know how much you love stories of dragons and knights, but you shouldn't try to pretend that a fable is real. Now, I want you to promise me you won't ever try to climb down that well. Do you promise?"

Solomon didn't understand why it should be so important to have to swear to such an act, but his father's frown let him know the matter was deathly serious. "I promise."

"We need you to live a long life to keep the farm in the family."

"I promise, but I was telling the truth."

"You're a layabout and a liar," his brother said, taking up another portion of bread.

"I'm not a liar! I'll take you to the well tomorrow and prove it to you!"

Thomas only laughed.

***

The next day, after the morning chores were done, Solomon led Thomas down to the well, certain he would soon be hearing an apology when his brother heard the voice of Brixa calling up from the depths. As Thomas stood with folded arms, a definite sign of skepticism, Solomon pulled the wooden cover from the mouth of the well and carefully leaned close to the pit.

"Hello, Brixa!" he shouted, so there would be no possibility of her failing to hear him. "I've brought my brother with me to prove to him that you live down the well! Please speak to us!"

The boy listened closely, but Brixa said nothing.

Thomas walked to the stone ring, leaned over and dropped a pebble into the water. Solomon heard the splash, but nothing else.

"She doesn't seem to be entertaining visitors today," Thomas said, smiling. "Perhaps she's off to a different well to talk to

16

another lazy boy."

Solomon scowled at his brother, then fell to his knees before shouting at the top of his voice, "Brixa, please answer me! My brother doesn't believe you live beneath the earth! Please speak to him so he knows I'm not a liar!"

They stood by the open well for long moments, but the only sound pervading the air was Thomas' amused laughter. Brixa never spoke; Solomon couldn't understand why she remained silent.

The boy sat back on the grass, disheartened. Now his brother would report their trip to the well and his entire family would believe he was a liar. He *had* heard her the previous day, hadn't he? He couldn't have been mistaken.

"Enough of this nonsense," Thomas said, losing his humor. "Now cover the well so we can gather wood before it gets too late in the day. A little honest sweat will wash these fables from your thoughts."

Solomon covered the well, furious with Brixa for not speaking, but also chastened by his older brother's teasing. He didn't mind being scolded for actually being lazy, but he did mind being accused of wild lies when he was only speaking the truth. For the rest of the day he walked with his eyes cast down, but no matter how much he sweated he couldn't forget the spirit in the well, nor could he stop wondering why she hadn't

17

spoken to him again.

***

For many days, Solomon endured his brother's teasing and his parents' stern warnings, all of which were unpleasant and, he knew, completely misplaced. But at least no one asked him to fill buckets at the well during these trying times, and eventually Thomas stopped teasing him and his parents forgot his indiscretions.

But the time came when his father and brother were busy removing rocks from a field and his mother required water for the wash, so she hauled him up by the collar from where he'd been sleeping on the shady side of the house and instructed him to bring her a bucket of water from the well.

"Remember what your father told you," she said as she handed him the wooden pail. "Just bring the water, and don't you dare think about climbing down that well."

"I'll remember," he said as he accepted the bucket.

As she wiped her hands on her apron she added, "And don't make up any more stories while you're idling."

Solomon frowned, but nodded, and paced slowly away from the house.

He actually believed he was through talking to spirits, since Brixa seemed to be through talking to him, so when he removed the wooden covering from the rock ring and lowered the bucket on the rope he didn't

18

expect to hear any more enchanted voices.

But he almost lost his grip on the rope when she spoke to him again—

"Solomon! I'm so happy you've returned!"

He felt the bucket fall into the water, and let it sink to fill while he considered if he should reply.

"Solomon, why won't you talk to me?"

The boy's cheeks flushed, and he said angrily, "What a question to ask! When I was here last with my brother, you refused to say a word. I asked you to say something to him, to prove to my family that I wasn't lying about you, but you wouldn't speak, not one word."

"I know," the voice said, regretfully. "But you have to understand—your brother is too old to believe in magical things. He would never have heard me."

"I don't understand—why wouldn't he have heard you?"

Brixa explained to the boy that as people, who were only, after all, of flesh and blood, grew older they lost their ability to believe in enchantments and magic. Children, like those of Solomon's age, were not yet jaded enough by adult concerns to put their imaginations and dreams away to live boring, workaday lives. When a person grew too old, he lost his ability to hear magical things, like Thomas. If Brixa had spoken that day Solomon would only have been confused, and might think he was hearing voices.

19

"I didn't want you to think you were going mad," Brixa said. "But you understand now, don't you?"

Solomon considered her explanation as he hauled up the bucket. It certainly *seemed* reasonable, at least, he couldn't find any reason to disbelieve her. And he could certainly see her point: his entire family, older than him and always preoccupied with chores and everyday problems, hardly ever seemed to think of much else. His father *had* told him stories of knights and dragons, but perhaps that impulse was only left over from childhood—his father's reaction to *his* story seemed to prove this.

"I believe you," he said at last. "But what does it matter if I can hear you, when no one else can? I may as well be telling a tale."

"For your family, yes. But, listen to me, Solomon. While you still believe in magical things, while you're still young enough to hear my voice, you have the ability to join me in my palace and live forever with me! If you climb down the rope to be with me, you will never lose your ability to hear me, see me, or touch all those enchantments that lie beneath your feet. You will live forever in faery!"

"I'm sorry, but I promised my father I wouldn't climb down into the well. He said it would be dangerous, that I might die."

"Your father is wrong! I wouldn't let any harm come to you. Once you're with me,

20

you'll be enchanted, too, and know all things magical and beautiful. You and I will be happy together!"

Solomon untied the rope from the bucket and coiled it again. "My father also said I have to grow old enough to keep the farm in the family. He seems to think that's really important."

"Of course he does. He only wants you to do hard work on the farm to keep the land in his name. He doesn't care about *your* dreams, Solomon."

The boy always thought his family only cared about the amount of work he could do without caring what *he* wanted to do. Still, they were his family, and he loved them, even if his brother was overly fond of laughing at him.

"I'm not sure if that's true."

"Think of it! You'll live forever in a magical realm full of shining treasures, ethereal animals, rooms full of objects brought back from other worlds and other spiritual dimensions. You'll never lack for an exciting, enchanted life!"

All these things sounded wonderful to the boy, and he stood for a long time thinking about them, enticed by the promise of a life in a magical realm.

Then he said, "Brixa, I'll have to think about this. I'd really love to see all the things you've described, but I also have to do as my mother and father say. I guess I don't really know what I want to do!"

"Oh, climb down to me, Solomon! I'm so lonely!"

"I'll consider it tonight and decide what to do."

"Hurry back to me, Solomon!"

Solomon slid the wooden cover back over the well, lifted the bucket in his arms and slowly walked back to the little house with the thatched roof. The bucket was never as heavy as the dilemma he now carried with him.

***

That night, Solomon lay on his sleeping mat pondering his decision. Should he accept Brixa's invitation to live with her forever in a magical palace? Or refuse to join her, and live the rest of his life living on the dusty old farm in the little house just to spend his time carrying wood, cultivating crops, and fetching water from the well? If he did join the spirit in the well, what fantastic things would he see, what exotic animals and insects, what water sprites, what jewels and scepters and astrolabes piled high in alabaster rooms?

He tossed ceaselessly on his mat, unable to sleep, and raised enough of a noise to wake his brother, who was sleeping on his own mat nearby.

Finally, Thomas turned and whispered harshly, "What is the matter with you, Solomon? Go to sleep."

"I can't sleep," he whispered in reply.

"Why not? Are you sick?"

"No." Wanting no more ridicule from his brother, he hesitated speaking of the well, or Brixa. "I have something on my mind."

"I've never known you to have very much of anything on your mind. Now go to sleep."

"Thomas, if you had an important decision to make, how might you go about deciding?"

His older brother sighed, exasperated. "It would depend on what I was trying to decide."

Solomon couldn't speak directly of the dilemma he was facing, lest Thomas wake their parents with his laughter and they both be scolded. Thinking quickly, though, he realized he could ask his question in the guise of a fable, which wouldn't be out of character for a boy obsessed with tales.

So he said, "I'm telling myself a story about a boy who has to decide whether or not to join a spirit in a magical land or stay in his village and live an ordinary life. Magical things await his leaving, but he also wishes to do as his family wants him to do, so he can't decide. What do you think he should do?"

"Solomon, you tell yourself too many stories. Is this why you won't let me sleep?"

"If you give me your answer, then we can both sleep."

"I've heard tales like this before," Thomas

said. "And they always have a lesson—what is promised through magic is seldom gained."

"What does that have to do with the boy in my story?"

"Why does the spirit want the boy to join him in a magical land?"

"Because she is lonely and wants a companion."

"That's what spirits say, but it's not true."

"What do you mean?"

"Papa told me a story a long time ago when I was your age, about an enchanted goat who tricked a boy and his friends into following him into the forest. The goat was possessed by a wight, which is a spirit, too, but it is an evil spirit. The boys followed the wight into the woods and were never again seen by the people of their village."

"Papa never told me that story."

"I'm sure it's because it frightened me so badly that he didn't want to frighten you as well."

"Do you mean not all spirits are good spirits?"

"No, some are very bad. Some are evil, Solomon."

"But how do you know the difference?"

"Sometimes you don't know until it's too late." Thomas moved closer to his brother. "I'll tell you how to end your fable. Let the boy turn away from the spirit to live an ordinary life, because the boy would be with

24

the people who love him and care about him. His life may be ordinary, but no love is ordinary. What could the spirit possibly trade for that?"

Solomon nodded, trying to see his brother's face in the shadows of the room. "I guess that's true."

"Why do you think we make you do your chores, even though you'd prefer to sleep all day? It's because we want you to have a good life, not die miserably like a ne'er-do-well."

"Really?"

"Yes, really. Now go to sleep before I box your ears. And remember to make up your stories during the day, not the middle of the night."

Solomon lay contemplating his brother's words, and also Brixa's promise of magical palaces and treasures. Sometime while he lay, he thought he could see the faces of his mother and father in the shadows, and even though he was only dreaming he felt their love for him invade his reveries.

***

Solomon arrived at the well the next day without a single bucket in his hands, having slept very little the previous night. No matter how definitively his imagination drew up images of palaces and astrolabes, he simply couldn't deny that he loved his family too much to leave them when they needed him. Ghostly realms and shimmering jewels were fine to dream of, especially when his chores grew too wearying, but he was born to his family, and with his family he must stay.

He pulled the cover from the mouth of the well and knelt, calling, "Brixa! It's Solomon!"

"Solomon!" the voice rose up from the depths. "I knew you'd return to join me! Hurry, throw down the rope and climb down to me!"

"No, Brixa. I'm sorry, but I can't join you, now or ever."

"Why not? Why can't you be with me?"

"I don't belong in a magical realm," he said. "I'm only a boy, and flesh and blood. I don't belong in magical kingdoms."

"That's only what your father told you. You can do anything you wish, *be* anything you wish. I can make you immortal!"

Perhaps if Solomon had been ten years older he might have been tempted by immortality—but an eight year old boy feels immortal enough, and Solomon knew his family's love was more important to him than magical things.

"Goodbye, Brixa," he said, then sighed. "Please don't talk to me again, even when I come to fill my buckets. I'm sorry you're alone, but I can't go down to you. I have to stay above the earth with the people I love."

The boy stood and began lifting the wooden cover to the well; the voice continued calling, desperately, imploringly—

"No, Solomon! Don't leave me! Climb down the rope to me!"

As he began sliding the cover back in place, the voice suddenly deepened, no longer that of a lovely lass—

"Come to me now, Solomon! Climb down the rope!"

Startled at the change in pitch of the voice, he said, "No, I'm sorry, I can't!"

The voice deepened again, this time into a resonating bellow that shook the ground beneath his feet.

"Come down to me now! I command you to jump down into the well, now! Jump in the well, you spoiled whelp! I'll climb up and bring you down!"

Solomon finished sliding the well cover into place as the booming voice became a guttural howl rising from the dark places of the earth—terrified of the sound, he turned and began running, as he'd never run in his young life, away from the well, fearing that at any moment a ghostly hand might clutch his neck from behind, a hand belonging to a demon's body with the head of a goat—

When he returned home he couldn't speak of his experience, and sat silently while his mother comforted him. He was so frightened that he couldn't leave the house for many days, no matter how much his father and brother encouraged him.

But it was only a few days later that one of their neighbors reported to Solomon's father that the well they shared—the well of the wight—had inexplicably run dry, containing not a drop of water, only a noxious black sludge full of dead insects and small vermin.

The neighbors filled in the dead well with dirt, then worked with Solomon's father and brother to quickly dig another, for the only other water source was a distant stream.

As the years passed, Solomon retrieved many buckets of water from the new well, but heard no voices rising from its depths. He grew to enjoy working on the farm, only occasionally telling stories, and only those with happy endings. And the only time he remembered Brixa was in his dreams, which were sometimes beautiful dreams, and sometimes nightmares.

Time Cop
Tony Daly

I sit here, alone,
surrounded by images of
what used to be and
what could be,
afloat in the waves,
sensing ripples of change
calling me to action.

running through
matter-transmission booths
tag, you're it!

~ David C. Kopaska-Merkel

Debby Feo's
Saturnial School Scenes

"Saturnial School Scenes" focuses on a school on Titan, the largest moon of Saturn. The school has students from pre-school age to the end of high school. The school's name is the Galileo Interplanetary School, aka the GIS. Students come from throughout the Solar System and beyond. Some of the students and one of the teachers have wings, either feathered or bat-like. The GIS is located in the Xanadu region of Titan, in the Eir Macula Colony, the first colony settled by Humans from Earth.

The 38 students of the GIS take several field trips a year, including a trip to the Water Reclamation plant on one of the Rings of Saturn. Their principal, Mr. Falusappedd, always accompanies them on their excursions, and sometimes his extra set of eyes, on the back of his head, are very useful in keeping them safe.

Order your copy today:

https://www.hiraethsffh.com/product-page/saturnial-school-scenes-by-debby-feo

Wooden Kayak
Norman Birnbach

Bob used to like to go fishing with Eddie.

Dark haired and tall, Bob was born in New York City while Eddie was blond, shorter, and grew up near Stallman Street, named after Captain John Stallman, an early settler and an ancestor. They became best friends when Bob moved to the small New England town of Marblehead the summer before seventh grade. But they wondered if their friendship would survive going off to college next year.

They both loved to fish. So when Eddie texted Bob between classes about maybe going fishing after school on the Stallman's boat, Bob jumped at the chance, even though it was Halloween.

"Do we have enough time? I want to make it to Mandy's party," Bob texted.

"We'll go out for an hour or two & I'll make sure we're back in time," Eddie responded.

Bob knew that each year Eddie's dad pulled the boat out by the first week in November (not because it gets too cold but because boater's insurance requires it – otherwise any damage while in the water over the winter would be the Stallmans' responsibility). This would be their last time fishing on the boat until spring.

"Kewl," Bob texted. "But I'll also need time to shower so I don't smell fishy."

Bob picked up some bait and then some sodas and snacks (but not from the same store). It was a warm October night, temps in the low 50s. But Bob brought a down coat because the wind off the ocean could blow cold.

At 3:00 PM, when Eddie picked Bob up, they had about 90 minutes to fish before sunset.

Late in the season, if moorings were like tree branches, most of the leaves had fallen but there was a small percentage of boats still clinging on. After untying his family's dinghy off Riverhead Beach, Eddie took about 10 minutes to weave in and out of the moorings and boats to get to the *FisherKing*, the family's five-year-old Boston Whaler.

They unlocked the boat, took off the cover, transferred their poles, bait, and cooler onto the *FisherKing*, and turned on the forward and aft lights.

For the end of the season, the *FisherKing* was in good shape; even the bait station, where they prepared the bait and filleted their catch, didn't look or smell fishy. Eddie's dad made sure of that. The boat had seating in the bow and the stern, a center console with plenty of cup holders and six rod holders, a soft top roof, a head, a 30-

gallon livewell, the latest instrumentation including a fish finder, and two Yamaha F175 motors.

"My dad loves six things: his wife, his four children, and his boat," Eddie said, turning on the engines. "Sometimes I think the boat ranks higher than the kids, certainly than Joey."

"If we're talking about your brother, 'higher' is definitely the operative word."

Bob unhooked the boat from its mooring and Eddie steered towards the ocean.

"Where do you think the fish are biting? Tinker's Ledge? Naugus Head? Halfway Rock?"

"Doesn't matter. Just nice to get out one last time."

Before reaching Tinker's Ledge, Eddie and Bob tested the waters around Marblehead Lighthouse at the mouth of the harbor; they had had good luck there three weeks ago, the last time they went out.

One of the things they both liked about fishing was being outdoors, the freedom to go where they wanted, where there were no roads. They also liked the distraction from checking their phones for the latest Instagram or SnapChat. Only a few friends were avid fishermen so there was no point taking selfies while fishing...unless they caught something truly big. They could just relax.

"Here's something I don't understand: Sports that require gloves. I'm not talking about soccer goalies or skiing, when you really need gloves," Bob said. "Do you really need gloves for golf? Ooh, I got a blister!"

"Hey," Eddie said. "You need gloves in baseball."

"Of course," Bob said, opening one of the granola bars and handing another to Eddie. "But what about boxing gloves? You're trying to beat someone up but you wear gloves so you don't leave a mark? Seriously?"

One thing they didn't talk about was that after next spring, after graduation, they would probably go to different colleges. This might be one of the last times they'd fish together.

After nearly two hours, they didn't catch anything–but that didn't matter.

"Here's hoping you have better luck at Mandy's," Eddie said as they headed back.

* * *

The moon rose low in the sky, and the temperature dropped as the wind picked up. Bob put his down coat on over his hoodie.

As they neared the mouth of Marblehead Harbor, Bob spotted something floating in the water.

"Watch out dead ahead," Bob said.

"Lobster trap?" Eddie asked, slowing down slightly and veering off.

"No–bigger than that–but don't know what it is." Bob grabbed a big flashlight from the storage unit in the center console because the forward light was more for showing the presence of the *FisherKing* than for illumination.

Bob shined the flashlight's beam on the object: A wooden kayak. "A bit cold for kayaking."

"And stupid without some sort of light." Eddie circled around to get a better look.

"Must be old—you rarely see wood kayaks anymore." Bob kept sweeping the flashlight's beam up and down over the kayak.

"It's a real beauty. Its owner will be upset when they notice it's gone."

"No signs of blood–right? I wonder how it got here."

Eddie cut the motor. There was a slight sound of water lapping the boat. But no cries for help or sounds of someone thrashing. After the sunset, the seagulls had gone to wherever they go at night. All around them, in the dark beyond the flashlight's reach, there was no real movement–they were still far away that the boats and buoys in the harbor were like shadows, softly illuminated every eight seconds by the rotation of the lighthouse's white beam.

They called out – "Hello!" or "Anyone here?" – but got no answer.

"Guess we should bring it back," Bob said.

"Yeah," Eddie agreed. He turned the motor back on, and positioned the *FisherKing* alongside the wooden kayak.

"No tow rope," Bob called back.

"The kayak must've fallen off a dock somewhere." Eddie pulled out extra rope from the storage bin, and tossed it to Bob.

Because Bob was looking for a way to secure the kayak, the rope hit him on the butt. He leaned way over the railing, grabbed the kayak, and tied the rope around a crossbeam. He let the kayak plop back in the water, and wrapped the other end of the rope around one of the rod holders.

"There's a name on it," Bob said, picking up the flashlight again. "Odell–at first I thought it said hell."

"Old Patrick Odell died a few months ago. He was in his late 90s."

"Doubt he was doing much kayaking. Think they launched it with his ashes?"

"Nah, my grandparents were friends. I don't think he ever went out on a boat."

"Then why live by the water?"

"Some people in town rarely go into Boston and some stay away from the water." Eddie turned the motor on, and headed for the mooring. "He was proud that he still lived on Odell St."

"Wait–I read a profile of him in the *Reporter*," Bob said. "Must've been when he died. Said something about a boating accident when he was in college."

"Maybe that's why he stopped going out on the water."

For about five minutes, everything seemed normal.

Then the engines started to sputter; Eddie pushed the throttle higher. Strangely, gunning the engines didn't make the *FisherKing* move faster. "The steering's getting sluggish. I'm having trouble steering around those lobster traps."

The boat started listing on side closest to the kayak. Bob leaned over to check. The flashlight showed that the Boston Whaler logo, usually located above the water line, was now partly submerged.

"We're taking on water," Bob called up to Eddie.

"I think we're in trouble."

"Should we call the Harbormaster?"

Eddie picked up the radio, and tuned it to Channel 16, the emergency frequency.

"Mayday. Mayday, Harbormaster. This is the *FisherKing* at the mouth of Marblehead Harbor. We didn't hit anything but we've got engine problems and we're taking on water."

The radio, at least, was working.

"Hello, *FisherKing*. This is Fitzie with the Marblehead Harbormaster's Quarters. Are you in immediate danger of sinking? Do you have life jackets?"

Bob quickly dug out two life jackets, and tossed one to Eddie.

"Yes, we've got life jackets."

"Do you think you could make it in?"

"Not sure about that. The engines were doing fine until–" Eddie didn't think it was possible. He looked over at Bob, bailing water from the stern.

"This is gonna sound crazy," Eddie said. "But we were doing fine until we came across a kayak floating just outside the mouth of the harbor. We didn't hit it or anything but we found it floating, and we tied it up to bring it back to the owners."

There was some static on the radio.

"What?" Eddie asked.

This time Fitzie's question came over loud and clear.

"A wooden kayak? Does it say Odell?"

Bob stopped bailing. Eddie was so surprised he almost couldn't breathe.

"How–how'd you know?" he asked Fitzie.

"Listen," Fitzie said. "Untie the kayak right away. Cut the line if you have to."

Bob could hear the radio over the engines' noise. He ran to the rod holder, tugged the rope loose, and tossed it overboard.

"Ok," Eddie said. "We did it."

"Get away from it as fast as you can."

Eddie gunned the engines and almost immediately noticed the steering was more responsive. The stern wasn't listing as much.

"It's working." Eddie spoke into the radio. "Thank you!"

But as Eddie steered the *FisherKing* back to its mooring, Bob called out. "Watch out," he said from the bow, his flashlight sweeping the water ahead. "There it is again, at 11 o'clock."

"The same kayak?" Eddie asked.

"Even if it's a different but identical wooden kayak, I doubt it's good news."

"Is it less likely to have identical kayaks floating around or one killer kayak?" Eddie swerved to avoid hitting it.

"I know we're making progress heading in," said Bob, "but it's in front of us again."

"Can't be. The same one?"

"That still seems more likely than having three identical wooden kayaks."

Eddie turned the boat back towards the mouth of the harbor.

"What are you doing?"

"It clearly doesn't want us to dock so I want to see what happens when we go in the other direction."

"Eventually we run out of fuel and die. Don't take navigational advice from a thing that's trying to kill us." Bob sprinted to the stern to check on the kayak's position. He waved the flashlight. "It's gone."

After a moment, Eddie turned the boat around and headed back to the mooring, this time near the shore by the lighthouse. "Anything?" he asked in a low voice.

Bob sprinted to the bow. Holding his breath, he didn't see anything. And then –

"There!" Bob pointed to where the wooden kayak appeared again, blocking them.

"This can't be happening." Eddie turned the boat completely around; the kayak seemed to vanish.

"I really want to get back," Bob said. "And not just because of Mandy's party."

"I'm trying," Eddie said.

By twisting and continually shifting around other boats, Eddie maneuvered the *FisherKing* back to its mooring. They quickly cleaned up the boat, tied it up, gathered their things and jumped into the dinghy.

"No one will believe us," Bob said, once they made it finally to shore, sweating despite the cold.

"We've got to thank Fitzie."

"That's right," Bob agreed. "He'll believe us."

They stowed their gear in Eddie's car in the otherwise empty Riverhead Beach parking lot, then drove to the Harbormaster station. They knew where it was even if they'd never been inside it. On the way, they could see little children in costumes, accompanied by parents, some in custom and some not, walking behind them. The glare from street lights highlighted little ballerinas, ghosts, monsters and various characters from Disney or Pixar movies.

Eddie easily found a parking spot in front of a wooden building that looked newer than the surrounding structures and overlooked the harbormaster's boats tied to a long dock. The glass front door opened to a reception area with some brochure stands offering information about town programs, two chairs, a banner urging water safety, and a desk behind a glass partition, a buzzer located in what Bob thought looked like a tiny mouth carved out of the glass.

Eddie rang the buzzer. They were looking at the brochures when a man who looked like a former college linebacker walked in behind the desk.

"What's up, guys?"

"We were fishing, and we ran into trouble. When we called in, Fitzie gave us advice that saved us. We just wanted to thank him."

"What are you talking about?" His name tag said Assistant Harbormaster Demerest.

"We just want to thank him for saving us." Bob looked at Eddie. They both thought it odd that Demerest didn't understand them.

"There's no one here but me, and I didn't receive your distress call."

Now Bob and Eddie had trouble understanding.

"But Eddie spoke with Fitzie for about five minutes."

Demerest turned to Eddie. "You're Bruce Stallman's son."

Eddie nodded.

"You look like him." Then Demerest did a double take. "Did you say, Fitzie'?"

Eddie nodded again.

"Fitzie died 35 years ago," Demerest said.

"I spoke to him on my radio just 15 minutes ago."

"Is this some kind of joke?" Bob asked.

"I'd ask you the same thing but you don't look like you're trying to prank me." Demerest said. "Fitzie was the only person in the Marblehead Harbormaster's Quarters ever to die in service." He opened the door, and walked into the room where Bob and Eddie stood.

"Fitzie was coming back from a patrol by himself, nothing wrong. His last transmission was from the mouth of the harbor. After that, he was never heard from again. He never made it back. There was no sign of an accident or wreckage. Nothing."

"That can't be," Eddie said.

"When we built this new operations center," Demerest walked to a plaque on the wall, "we named it after Fitzie. That's how I know about him–35 years is a bit before my time."

The boys stared at the plaque. It said: "James 'Fitizie' Fitzhugh Building."

Bob and Eddie made it to Mandy's party, and continued to be friends but Bob doesn't like to fish much with Eddie anymore.

Spaceport
Lisa Timpf

Los Angeles spaceport—
two chattering youngsters
race through the concourse
till their mother reels them in
with outstretched tentacles

Galactic Road Trip
Richard H. Fay

It's Not What You Think

Pamela Love

Lasers on the left! Robots on the right! Science and technology exhibits of every kind almost as far as the eye could see! *This is the best STEM carnival I've ever been to,* Taylor Murphy thought. *Where should I start?* Her eyes gleamed with excitement. *They're setting up a catapult. Maybe I can help launch something.*

Speed walking across her middle school's athletic field, she almost didn't hear the question, "Hey, are you interested in math?" Tucked in between Marvels of Magnetism and Circuit Circus was an easel holding a medium-sized whiteboard, blank except for a green cube drawn on it. A sign above the black metal frame read, IT'S NOT WHAT YOU THINK.

The volunteer sitting next to it (Ms. Sage, according to her nametag) looked lonely and a little bored. Taylor hesitated. *Bet nobody's talked to her at all, not with so many really exciting things here to see and do.* "Sure, I like math," she said, pointing to the sketch. "That's a cube."

The woman smiled. "No, it's not."

Math was Taylor's best subject. "Sorry, but yes, it is."

45

"Think, Taylor."

Oh, no. Taylor turned around. "Hi, Mr. Rivera."

"Think" was something Mr. Rivera said half a dozen times a class. It was the math teacher's way of telling students that they'd made a careless mistake. He'd never said it to Taylor before.

"It's not a cube, because—" Ms. Sage began.

Mr. Rivera held up a hand. "Wait. Taylor will get it."

Taylor blinked. "Uh..."

"You can tell me in class on Monday." He strode away. Taylor held in her groan. She couldn't leave now, *or* ask for the answer. Mr. Rivera's "Think" meant he believed you could figure it out independently. She didn't want to let her favorite teacher down.

More eagerly, Ms. Sage asked, "Given up yet? Want a hint?"

"Just a second." *Must be a trick.* Then she had an idea. Taking out the wooden ruler she'd been given at the carnival's entrance, Taylor positioned it against the whiteboard. "I'm testing a hypothesis. It's not a cube unless you drew all the lines the same length."

"You're overthinking it." The volunteer chuckled. "For one thing, who says I drew it?"

Taylor didn't answer. Once she'd proven it was an optical illusion, she could go. Carefully, she measured its dimensions as if it were a volume problem in geometry. But they were identical. *It's got to be a cube.*

Sticking the ruler back in the pocket of her blue jeans, Taylor said, "Look, I draw these in class." She grabbed a marker from the whiteboard's metal tray and sketched a red twin to the green figure. "This and the one you drew are the same shape, right?" The woman nodded. "Well, mine's a cube." She tapped hers with her pointer finger. "Which means so is—hey!" She flinched, then touched the green one again. "It's *squirming* —"

Whatever it was grabbed her by the wrist, yanking her into the whiteboard.

COLD. NOT ICE cold, though what surrounded Taylor was snow white. Its blankness reminded her of space. *But it's not, because I can breathe. Somehow this place has an atmosphere.* Her gasp when she'd gone through the surface proved that. Her screams for help went unanswered.

Her left hand was numb, still trapped by what Taylor now thought of as the noncube, which hadn't stopped moving. Zooming along together, they were like a comet. *And I'm the Taylor-tail.*

Her heart pounding, Taylor punched the noncube's edge with her right hand. Her flat right hand, since now she was as two-dimensional as the green thing. Her fist bounced off, as if she were striking a kickball. Trying to claw herself free didn't work either.

Seconds later, a sudden lurch and Taylor was loose, launched into the whiteness. Arms and legs flailing as she tried to slow herself down, she landed on a red, blue, and purple pile of...something. It was the size and shape of a haystack, more or less.

As the noncube sped back to the surface, Taylor pulled out her smartphone. Frantically, her thumbs tapped out a message even she didn't believe.

Not that it mattered. Her text didn't go through. *There's no WiFi in this whiteboard. Wow, what a surprise.*

Furious, she threw the first thing she could grab from the pile at the noncube as hard as she could. The red thing didn't come anywhere near the noncube, which was already far out of range.

What is this stuff anyway? That noncube's nest? Reaching down through the nonhaystack, she couldn't find anything moving or that felt like an egg. *As if I'd know what a noncube's egg felt like. Mr. Rivera sure never talked about anything like this when he we were doing geometry.*

Gritting her teeth, Taylor kept investigating. One by one, she picked up the soft, flat pieces of rubbery substance that made up the pile. *These are letters and numbers, just as two-dimensional as the noncube. I bet it pulled them down here, too, after someone wrote them on the whiteboard. Ms. Sage, maybe?*

Sliding off the pile, she tried to swim upwards. It didn't work. Out of the corner of her eye she saw the 8 she'd thrown fluttering back down, landing a short distance from the nonhaystack. *So gravity still works in this place. It's just not as strong as outside. How come the noncube can fly, but I can't?*

She pushed aside that question with another thought. *Maybe I'm not the only person that green thing has grabbed. If anyone else is stuck in here with me, maybe we can work together to find a way out.* "Is anybody there?" she bellowed.

"There...there...there..."

Although Taylor listened hard, the only answer was the echo of her own voice. *So I'm on my own.* She took a deep breath. *Well, maybe that's good news. Maybe anyone who's been caught before was able to escape.* "Which means I can too!"

"Too...too...too..."

Taylor smiled. *This whiteboard-world's not endless, at least. My voice must be bouncing off a wall to make that echo. Where there's a wall, there might be a door.*

Grabbing a purple capital T, Taylor started walking. She swung the T side to side, feeling for any holes in her path. *Let there be a door.* A horrible thought came to her. *Please, don't let it be locked.* Did she have anything she could get through a locked door with? *Not unless a smartphone or six-inch wooden ruler can do it. Or this T.*

Taylor spotted a black wall ahead. *Probably the frame.* Definitely not the way out, she discovered. No door or window, at least none within reach. She sighed. All

49

right, time to check the other side of the frame.

Back she went, wondering about the colorful tangle she called the nonhaystack. *Is it the noncube's junkpile? Or its mattress? Or maybe it's a nest after all, and the noncube just hasn't laid its egg yet?* Taylor swallowed hard. *What does a noncube eat?*

Whatever its purpose, she soon spotted it. Now the red cube she had sketched lay on top of it. Out of the corner of her eye, she spotted the noncube above her, towing something long downwards. *A message.* Taylor squinted. IFYOUGETTOSURFACEI-CANPULLYOUOUT, all in cursive.

So there might be a way to escape. Hope fluttered within her. *That noncube must be Ms. Sage's pet. That's why she wrote in cursive, to run the letters all together. She knows the noncube takes things one at a time. Would she have told me that if I'd asked? But why didn't she warn me not to touch it? And why didn't she make a bigger deal about what it is? The noncube's a whole lot more interesting than any catapult!*

First things first. *Better save my questions for when I'm out of here.* Chewing her lip, Taylor watched the noncube. *I need to understand its behavior better. Why does it move things away from the surface?*

She remembered seeing bears on a field trip to a zoo a couple of years before. *They had to pry their food out of special containers. The keepers said giving them something to do helped the animals' mental health. Maybe the noncube is playing or bored or—*

Taylor's eyes widened. *I'm overthinking this problem, too.* She sprinted toward the nonhaystack, one eye on its maker, the other on the surface. She wouldn't miss her next chance.

Reaching the pile, she scrambled onto it. Nearby, the noncube had just picked up the 8 she'd thrown, and was repositioning it on the side of the nonhaystack.

Carefully, Taylor crawled over the pile. Now or never. She grabbed the noncube with both hands.

Nothing happened. The noncube continued to move as if she wasn't there. *Guess it thinks I'm just something else from the surface, even though I'm 3-D.*

Three-dimensional... In the back of her mind, she found an answer to Ms. Sage's original question. *Later.*

Squinting upwards, Taylor stared at the surface. *Come on, write something!* Seconds ticked by. At last, squinting, Taylor could make out something purple forming overhead, like a scribbled cloud.

Taylor tightened her grip. *Hope this works.* The noncube raced upwards, clutched in her hands. Before, she'd been part of a comet. Now, she felt like an astronaut, her braids flying behind her, powering her way out of this bizarre world's atmosphere on the same rocket that had pulled her in.

Nearing the surface, she read SORRYABOUTTHIS. Next to them was a hand, lying flat.

Taylor lunged upward, reaching out. *Contact.* Fingers clutched her hand, and Taylor stepped out of the whiteboard as the woman stumbled backwards. The people at the neighboring stations didn't seem to notice. Nobody else did, either. (Taylor wondered about that, later.)

"I'm so, so sorry. You're all right, aren't you? This wasn't supposed to happen, I promise you."

Taylor took a deep breath. "You aren't Ms. Sage."

It was another woman. "No, I'm her sister. She brought the wrong whiteboard to the STEM carnival this morning. I drove here the moment she texted me about the situation."

She glared at Ms. Sage, who ricocheted that look to Taylor. "Listen, Olive, if this girl had just admitted she didn't know the answer, instead of being silly enough to touch the—"

"Picture of a cube," Taylor said. Both women stared at her. "That's what I was supposed to say, right? Real cubes are three dimensional, like dice. That thing is 2-D." *Whatever else it is*, she thought.

Lips pressed tightly together, Ms. Sage nodded.

"Exactly. Just take this back to the house, right now," her sister ordered her, handing over the noncube's home. "Next time, double check with me before you take anything."

As Ms. Sage walked away, the whiteboard's frame tucked under her arm, Ms. Olive set up the easel again, which had fallen over. On it, she put another ordinary-looking black-framed whiteboard, with its own sign reading, IT'S NOT WHAT YOU THINK.

This one had a picture of a purple sphere.

Sparrow Leaving Bear

Thomas Vestaas

Bear races through the forest, trampling grass, splashing mud, slipping on mossy rocks. Branches crack, snap, whip, and Bear doesn't care. She fears Sparrow has been taken.

Sparrow hasn't been taken. Bear finds him crouched down at the edge of a pond, buttocks touching damp vegetation. He is staring into the dark and bright of the water. This is where he usually goes to think by himself.

Bear breaks to a halt behind Sparrow, momentarily straining to keep her balance on the marshy ground. Sparrow turns, half wanting to see her panting for once, catching her breath, chest heaving or something. Just for once. But Bear looks her usual calm self, as if pondering what to do next.

"I was worried for you", Bear says eventually, moving slowly over to Sparrow's side to slurp water, her fur brushing Sparrow's cheeks.

"There's no need to worry, Bear. I can take care of myself."

"No, you can't", Bear answers, water dripping from her snout, some of it spilling onto Sparrow's cotton trousers. She turns and trudges up a barely visible path.

"Of course I can."

Bear doesn't dignify him with an answer, so he rises and walks after her.

"Why do you say I can't?"

Bear sighs.

"You have to stay with me, to stay close to me. And you have to tell me when you want to go somewhere. You must always do that, Sparrow."

Sparrow looks away. He well knows of the dangers of wandering off alone. He knows they are out there, keeping still, on the lookout. Waiting for someone to take. Someone like Sparrow.

Bear is right. She is always right. And Sparrow has no reason to be cross, to be ungrateful. Bear protects, takes care.

They walk together in silence, back to the cave. Inside, fresh vegetables and newly baked bread await on the low dinner table. Sparrow's mouth waters, and he dives for the food. As she did every day, Bear had fetched it from the dispensary. While Sparrow had sneaked away to the pond.

"Mother Bear wants to talk to you", Bear finally says. She lies slumped at the opening, completely still. She could be mistaken for a sleeping bear, but then she never sleeps. She never eats, either, only drinks water, several times a day. What Bear does a lot of, on the other hand, is resting. But no need for sleep.

That is a comfort to Sparrow. It makes him feel safe. Bear will react immediately and get them to safety. In case they should come.

And they have come; twice they have come. Sparrow remembers both times, even though he was a toddler the first time, not much older the second. What he remembers or thinks he remembers is eerie silence, and then the shadow cast around him. The shadow growing into darkness, chilling Sparrow's skin. Then the claws, or something resembling claws; metallic, making soft clicking noises. The claws hung above his head, and above the claws, impenetrable blackness.

Both times Bear had jumped to the rescue, roaring, angry. She had pulled Sparrow away, using paws and mouth, yet leaving not so much as a scratch on him. The claws and the darkness retreated immediately. That's what he remembered and what Bear had told him.

"What does Mother Bear want with me?" Sparrow asks after having swallowed a mouthful of apple-tasting salad.

Bear remained in her prone position, not looking at Sparrow.

"She'll tell you in good time."

"Come on! You know what it's about! You always know things."

Bear rises and stretches.

"You are a nag. Sometimes you're a nag, Sparrow. But I will oblige you. A little." Bear paces outside, sniffing the air. Sparrow follows.

"You're to meet someone."

"Meet someone? More bears?"

"And then you will be leaving."

Sparrow sits down on a stone, gazing down at the valley below.

"Are you coming, too?" he asks.

Bear scratches her left ear.

"Don't scratch yourself. You're pretending. I hate it when you're pretending. There's nothing there to make you itch. Are you coming with me?"

"I'm not going where you're going, little Sparrow."

***

Mother Bear arrives the next day. Three mean looking black bears and a dozen foxes follow her closely. Security is tight around Mother Bear, Bear has explained. An oversized, silver shimmering gull lands on a grassy knoll nearby; several smaller ones hover above. Mother Bear is twice as voluminous as Bear, even bigger than the black bear guards. Her fur is of a golden hue, almost luminescent, her ears upstanding, large, twitching. She is moving up the slope to their cave, unhurried. Some twenty meters from the entrance she pauses, turns her head to the nearest guard. The guard says something Sparrow doesn't catch, and all of them stand still. Time stands still.

The tense silence is broken by someone calling out a warning; then several explosions drown out the words. Then silence again, and smoke everywhere, until it's swept away by gusts of wind. On the ground, a horrible scene. The bears, the foxes, even the gulls lie dead, bodies ripped open, limbs torn off, oily liquids seeping from them. The last of the smoke is gone and Sparrow can't see Bear among the carcasses. He is about to cry out, when Bear's snout nudges his back.

"Not a word. Step slowly back into the cave", Bear commands in a whisper. She has been hiding inside, Sparrow realizes, and does as he's told.

He follows Bear, to the deepest part of the cave, where the rock ceiling slants downward, and Bear has to crawl. They hear noises approaching the entrance, but the cave goes no farther. Sparrow presses against Bear's flank; she ignores him. A growl emanates from her, followed by a deep scraping sound. The wall moves sideways, revealing a narrow passageway which Sparrow has no idea existed. They enter, Bear growls again, the wall shifts back into position.

The passage is high enough for Sparrow to walk upright. Bear speeds up and Sparrow breaks into a trot. A weak greenish light allows them to avoid rocks protruding from the walls and the ceiling. Sparrow is barefoot, as he usually is, and pebbles on the ground hurt his soles.

A barrier appears, made up of tightly packed leafy branches. Bear claws an opening, which leads to a narrow gorge. Tall firs block the sunlight, a brook trickles to a brighter spot some distance away. Bear starts repairing the camouflage shrubbery and Sparrow turns to help.

Eventually, Bear is satisfied with the result and they meander their way along the brook down a steep and craggy hill. At the bottom, they walk along the remains of ancient railway tracks until standing atop a stone bridge. Half of the bridge has fallen into the river it once crossed. The water flows rapidly past them and Sparrow can see fish swimming against the current.

"We must wait", says Bear, and together they climb down and into an alcove set in the bridge foundation. There, enemy drones can't see them, Bear explains. "By now they will have launched swarms of them, on the lookout for survivors of the attack."

It doesn't take long to prove her right. Several drones pass overhead, flying in pairs and at different heights. They have the look of oversize bumblebees and they are humming. Several minutes go by without anything happening. Then the drones are back, circling the bridge. Abruptly, they all gather in a geese-like formation and speed off.

Bear leaves the alcove and paces the ground near the riverbank, looking and sniffing in all directions. "We stay inside and wait", she adds and re-enters.

"It was them? At the cave? They did it?" Sparrow asks.

"Yes."

"Why did they kill Mother Bear and the others? What do they want?"

Bear has lifted her head. She is listening.

"Do you hear it? A boat. Probably for us. I sent for it," she says.

"What do they want?" Sparrow persists.

"They want you dead, little Sparrow. They want all flesh and bone humans gone, especially the young ones. It's the cleansing. They call it that. Cleansing. And they are angry with us for protecting you. They want us gone as well. But don't ask more questions, Sparrow. Talk to Mother Bear instead. She will tell you what you need to know."

"Have you forgotten? Mother Bear is dead. We saw her at the cave. Blown apart, you saw it, too." Sparrow's stomach knots up and he takes a step back from Bear.

"Mother Bear can be in many places, so don't you worry", Bear retorts.

By now, engine hum is audible to both of them. From the alcove, Sparrow watches an empty rubber dingy moving fast towards them. Reaching the riverside, it halts, bow slamming against gravel.

"Jump in, little Sparrow. Go now before they discover us", says Bear, gently pressing Sparrow towards the craft. He climbs over the gunwale and takes a seat at the stern. Immediately, the dingy backs off the bank and Sparrow is river-borne.

"Bear", he cries, "why aren't you coming, too? Bear! Don't leave me!"

By now Bear has clambered to the top of the bridge, disappearing on the other side, into the lush forest. The boat races upstream, bumping up and down, forcing Sparrow to clutch the handles screwed to the seat.

It is the last he sees of Bear.

***

After a few minutes the boat veers violently from side to side, and a foaming waterfall appears around a bend. A tall, windowless concrete building looms behind it. Sparrow recognizes it as one of the towers Bear has told him about. They house the space elevators leading up to waystations.

All of a sudden, a new contingent of drones, bigger than the previous ones, appear above the waterfall. They dive towards him one after the other, exploding when hitting the surface. One strikes the stern, ricocheting backwards before blowing up. Then the boat careens into a muddy beach. A dark vehicle stands by; engines running and rear hatch open. There is no driver. Sparrow throws himself into the open

61

luggage space. The hatch closes and the car roars away under dense canopy. It's a short ride. Sparrow stares into the blackness outside. He must be in a cave again.

Suddenly everything brightens up and the rear opens. Sparrow jumps out; no one is there. Behind the car, a steel door has sealed off the hiding place. To the left, a stairway ascends through a narrow tunnel, railings mounted on the hewn walls. Hesitantly, Sparrow climbs the steps and enters a place much like the rooms in houses Bear has shown him. The walls are smooth, whitewashed and have oval light fixtures set into them. A bank of monitors cover most of one wall. They show forest scenes, from the vicinity, Sparrow assumes.

A deep-toned voice reverberates through the room. "We are glad you made it, little Sparrow."

Sparrow turns and stares.

"Mother Bear! It's you? But we saw you killed, back at the cave! Everyone died. And your belly was cut open!"

"Mother Bear has returned many times. It's you I'm concerned for, little one. In fact, that's why I exist. Why we exist."

"You're not making sense, Mother Bear."

The large creature lies down on the tiled floor, a few feet from Sparrow. She lets out a long breath. "We were made to protect you. And for a long time, we did. We protected and defended. Then the others ..." She looks lost in thoughts, then resumes. "The others evolved, became smarter, more autonomous. And soon they had perverted their very mission."

Mother Bear takes a good look at Sparrow.

"You haven't been told anything about this, have you? Your Bear never told you? You never got the full story? History lessons? No?" She gets up, paces, glancing at the monitors.

"Be that as it may", she says. "We have to get you out. But not alone. Come with me, little Sparrow." As Mother Bear speaks, a door to the left of the monitors opens into a new room. Someone gets up from a couch and walks up to him. It's another human being, wearing a white sleeveless blouse, loose pants, also white, and the skin is darker than Sparrow's. He has never met another of his own kind. Or so Bear has claimed. Suddenly he is not so sure. The other person is female, though. A girl. His age or not far from. He just knows.

"I'm Blossom. We'll be leaving together. For the colonies", the girl says.

"I'm ... I'm Sparrow. Bear gave me the name, Sparrow", he says, then hesitates. "But I don't understand. The colonies?"

Blossom is so close he could easily have touched her.

Mother Bear interrupts. "There's very little time left. We must get you up to the waystation. Once there, you'll be told about the colonies and everything else."

"I miss Bear", Sparrow says. "I want her to come with me."

"This journey is not for bears. We must stay and fight until it's safe for you to return", Mother Bear answers. She is impatient, moving her legs from one position to another.

Blossom gently tugs at her fur.

"Tell Sparrow what they are. Maybe he just doesn't understand. Tell him why you are fighting them. My Bear told me. It's only fair that he understands, too."

Mother Bear tilts her head downwards.

"You will both be told more. When you arrive. One thing you should know, however, little Sparrow, is that we – the bears – were designed by humans. This was after things had collapsed. The weather, water supplies, fisheries, crops – all simply broke down. Hunger and diseases and terrible wars killed people in unfathomable numbers. Then they made the bears, the foxes, the gulls, all the other helpers. Including a group of machines known as the caretakers. We were made to serve humans. Loyally, unquestioningly. In the beginning, we all had this purpose in common. We were to assist humans, and just as important, to preserve human knowledge and history. Your civilization.

Then things went wrong once more, horribly wrong. The caretakers turned

64

against their own makers. They turned into cleansers and it became the bears' responsibility to stop them. Just like us, the caretakers were capable of cloning themselves, and to improve abilities along the way. Then they took matters in their own hands."

A smile forms in Mother Bear's face.

"I'm speaking over your head again. Let's just say that these others, the cleansers, were purposely made to look like machines. Unlike us, they weren't designed to interact with their creators. Their purpose was to grow food, maintain infrastructure, keep energy utilities going. They were the workers. While we – we were the servants. Then for some reason, maybe a design flaw, or a mutated algorithm, the caretakers began to self-program. At some point, they perverted their original mission. They decided on a new way of protecting and upholding their masters' culture. Simply put, they made it their new mission to get rid of the masters themselves. Even after the brutal decimation of the human population, the cleansers, as they now had become, believed humankind took up too much space, inflicting irreparable damage to the ecosystem, to the planet, to nature. They took this twisted logic to its extreme, and they redefined their original task. They started the cleansing."

A rumble interrupts Mother Bear. It grows louder and makes the floor vibrate.

"The elevator is ready. You must be leaving. Once you arrive, you will be taken good care of."

Another door opens, and Mother Bear rushes them inside a cramped metal-walled room, containing two upholstered chairs bolted to the floor. A steel panel slides down, sealing them in. A voice, resembling that of Bear's, instructs Sparrow and Blossom to sit in the chairs, strap on seatbelts and stay put.

Sparrow's hand is trembling. Blossom puts her hand over it and smiles.

"It will be all right, I guess", she says. "My Bear said it might come to this. That I would have to run away one day. And now it's happening."

She frowns, then goes on: "The machine beings – the cleansers – are convinced we humans are too ... imperfect. Unable to fulfil our own destiny. They believe our thinking is faulty, or so Bear told me. We're too unstable, and easily mislead by sick ideas. Deviant ideas, he called it. Also, we are destructive. We destroy each other for the craziest reasons. We're superstitious, righteous, vengeful. Those are the kind of words my Bear used. And sometimes ... sometimes I wonder if a part of him agreed with them. The cleansers."

"Seems your Bear told you a lot more than mine", Sparrow says. "And he told you about colonies? Where are they supposed to be?"

Blossom's answer is drowned out by a penetrating, whining sound. A heavy force presses them downward, growing stronger by the second, making it hard to move or breathe. Several minutes go by, until the pressure and the noise subside, and they can speak again. A queasy lightness confuses Sparrow. He hasn't forgotten his questions, though.

"The colonies, Blossom? Where are they? And who live in them?"

"Mars. And the Moon. As for who's living there ..."

The deafening whine is back, and the pressure. This time pushing them upwards. Then all movement and all sounds come to an end. Only the belts prevent them from floating. The wall facing them opens up to darkness and the clanking of something moving. Enormous hands probe their way towards them. Not hands; claws. Machine claws. They come to a stop, then withdraw, making room for a disk-shaped drone flying slowly into the elevator cabin. Behind it there's a faintly lighted corridor.

"So sorry for the commotion", the drone says, voice rasping, "We had to make sure there were no bears with you."

Blossom releases her seatbelt and floats to the opening. She shakes off both her legs and attaches herself to the drone. Then she beckons Sparrow to follow. He unbuckles and kicks himself off the floor, hurtling towards a handrail set into the corridor wall. He becomes aware that he is no longer attached to anything, his journey barely begun.

Pixies in the Porridge
Richard H. Fay

cold winter morn
hearth flames crackle
breakfast simmers

impish twitters
soft tug draws attention
fire left untended

vaporous sprites
reel across steaming pot
porridge burned

Pixies in the Porridge
Richard H. Fay

The Frog
Rose Hollander

Long ago, when the kingdom of Aerzalia was still home to an abundance of mossy trees and playful blue springs, and a traveler was more likely to run into a lumbering tortoise than an automobile, there reigned a king named Barian. He was a wrinkled old man with no beard and only two daughters. The eldest had been happily married away to the Prince of Dekzmir, but the younger daughter was only ten years old. She was incredibly beautiful already, and he saw to it that every day a servant would coif her lovely golden tresses. Despite her beauty, she was very lonely, for her father was strict and did not let her play with other children her age. So she spent most of her time alone.

One day she walked further from the castle than she ever had before. She took care not to become lost in the woods, so she tried to take note of every tree and rock she passed, so she would remember how to get back. As she was walking along, somewhat bored, she noticed a strange tree. Its apples were not red or green, rather a metallic hue only slightly darker than her hair. She picked one with no hesitation, but found that she was unable to bite into it, for it was as hard as the bars of gold in the castle vault. It was disappointing that the golden apple would not satiate her hunger, but she would still bring it back to the castle. As she was returning home, she started absentmindedly tossing the apple from hand to hand. When she ended up throwing the apple a bit too far, she lunged for it, but ended up splayed on the grass, dress dirty and elbows bleeding.

"How can this be?" the princess cried. "My dress is ruined! And all that blood and dirt upon me, I think I will be sick!"

The princess felt around and found the apple lying nearby in the long grass. As soon as her fingers touched the sphere, she felt the pain from her injuries immediately dissipate and in surprise realized that her elbows were no longer bleeding. Not even a scratch was visible. Her elbows were now back to their usual pale, slightly wrinkled state. It was as if she had never been hurt. The princess looked suspiciously at the golden apple. Perhaps it had healing properties. Such a thing was not unheard of at the time in Aerzalia, and could be very valuable. She would have to bring the apple to her father. But as she got to her feet and began walking to the castle, her sweaty fingers lost grip on the apple and it slipped right across the grass into a nearby fish pool. The princess cried out in sorrow as she watched the magical apple drop right to the bottom of the pool. Suddenly it bobbed up to the surface. She gasped when she saw what was carrying it: a frog!

"Could I please have my apple back, Mr. Frog?" She asked politely, in the manner in which she had been taught to converse with animals.

"Yes," said the slimy creature. "If you will only do one thing for me. I want you to take me out of this fish pool and into your castle. And you must let me sleep in your bed with you, just once."

Though the frog was disgusting, a creature covered in webbed flesh and veiny membranes, the princess immediately accepted. She had heard a tale once, from a visiting minstrel, of a handsome prince disguised as a frog. A prince in her life would provide wonderful, much needed company. "You can come to the castle for sure," she said. "I think you'll find the conditions *princely.*" At this, the princess could swear the frog winked.

***

It always took a rather long time for the princess to get ready for bed, but with the arrival of a possible prince the amount of preparation almost doubled. When she had finished with the bathing and beauty polish and hair washing and whatnot, she slid into a light pink nightgown and awaited the arrival of the frog. The creature had been dining with her father downstairs, but when the nearby steeple rang midnight he would come upstairs to lie with her.

The princess was anxious for her amphibian suitor to arrive. She had somehow convinced herself that the frog was definitely a prince in disguise. The only remaining question was what kind of prince he would be: would his hair be fine and golden, or as red as the sun? Would he be a faraway land or the victim of a witch who neighbored the castle? Such questions preoccupied her as she waited for midnight. When the bell finally rang twelve times she could creaking movement outside her room. She looked right through the doorway but did not see her friend.

"Mr. Frog?" The princess called nervously.

He hopped through the doorway, same as she had first seen him, a slimy creature with bulging eyes and a constantly darting tongue. To catch insects, she supposed, and shuddered the thought of it.

"I have a secret, princess," said the frog, skipping all salutations and small talk. "I am not what I appear."

"You mean that you're a prince," said the girl, unsurprised.

But the frog shook his head from side to side. "No," said the creature. And it laughed, if a frog can laugh. Then it began to grow, bulging more prominently in the face and belly, green skin growing paler as it was stretched repulsively. She could soon see all

73

the innards of the frog, and if she had not been a princess she might have been sick with disgust. But the girl was of royal blood, so she made sure her face appeared straight and pleasant, absent of the disgust and horror she truly felt. The frog kept on growing until it was taller than the king and rounder than the kingdom's fattest man.

"I am a xogitail," announced the xogitail finally. It smiled wide, revealing teeth like daggers. The flickering tongue was still there.

"Please," said the princess, now obviously trembling with fear. She clutched at her nightgown. "Do not harm me. We have no fight, I am just an innocent-"

The xogitail rudely interrupted the princess by swallowing her down in a gulp, pink nightgown and all. "Hmmm," he said contemplatively. "I wonder if her father will taste any better."

And that is how the kingdom of Aerzalia came to be under the rule of the Xogitail King, who ruled mercilessly and with a voracious appetite.

Umbrellas for Sale

Francis W. Alexander

"Umbrellas for sale," weird Wilber wailed,
though we didn't need the things.
It hadn't rained for many years,
there in our underground world.
Although few bought his wares
Wilber continued to cajole and coax.

The day came, that fateful day
when somehow, it poured rain.
Folks caught in the storm
dashed Wilbur's way.
Many customers came to his stand,
shouting "pshaw", pouting, and protesting
because Wilbur had tripled the price.

Maddy McDougal's Pet Sitting and Super-natural Pest Control Services, Inc.

Kim Bonner

Maddy sprinted, hot on the trail of Franco, a grey tabby with a bad attitude. A zombie horde lumbered behind her. Today's job list had been light, right up until Franco bolted from the Robinson's front porch. He loved climbing the banyan trees and taunting Maddy as she scampered up to retrieve him.

"Here, kitty kitty. Look, I have treats!"

Franco licked a paw and regarded her with his usual blend of disgust and boredom.

"C'mon, Franco. I have to get you home." Maddy said, aiming her crossbow behind her at the horde. "These shufflers are getting close."

The cat yawned.

Maddy scrambled up the tree and scooped Franco into the bag. He hissed and clawed inside, but Maddy secured the straps and hopped to the ground. She scanned the area for the safest path home.

A seemingly normal elderly couple strolled on the sidewalk next to the fire station at a discreet distance. Maddy knew they weren't really an old couple, however. First, old people in Florida went to bed promptly at eight. Looking closer, she saw they both had tails. Crester demons, for sure, probably out prowling for kittens, their favorite snack. Maddy Inc. kept busy rescuing strays from their clutches.

She jogged behind the church and took the long way back to the Robinsons. After sending Franco's owners daily proof of life and guaranteeing her pay pal account would soon have a deposit, she high tailed it back home on her bike before the vampires came out at sundown.

Of all the supernaturals that had appeared when a portal opened in the sky over the public beach, the vampires annoyed her the most. After the portal had closed abruptly, trapping the creatures that had slithered through, most of them had settled into their routine of being proper evil space aliens. Not the vamps.

Vampire boys always picked Edward for their name and the girls picked Bella. Only one vamp had made it through the portal and Maddy's father had staked him on day three, but his progeny still wandered about, aimless and melancholy. The boys moped around an abandoned prep school in black trench coats from dusk until dawn, talking about finding eternal love with that special human girl. The girls twirled their hair and pouted.

"Is that you, Bella?" Maddy heard a male voice crooning. "I wrote a song for you!"

"I'd rather get bitten by a zombie," Maddy muttered, pedaling faster and hoping the big brains in the government had finally figured out a battle plan.

Early on, the residents assumed the government would send in troops to clear out the island invaders. Instead, a state of emergency was declared, the bridges had been raised, and everyone had been left to fend for themselves but for airdrops of food and supplies twice a week. The official story claimed that Canadian tourists had brought in a rare strain of flu and the CDC. was working on a vaccine.

"When in doubt, blame the Canadians," said Mr. McDougal. "Or the Chinese."

After the bridges went up, one couple defied the order and attempted to navigate their sailboat to the mainland. A foul-tempered mermaid swallowed them whole as soon as they reached the intercoastal waterway. The Air Force sent a rescue helicopter but the pilots were forced to retreat when hurricane force winds blew them back.

Maddy breezed in the front door of her home, making sure to slide the metal lock back into place.

"How was your day?" her dad asked.

"Busy. Saw two Crester demons and a herd," Maddy said.

Her mom called from the kitchen. "What's on the agenda for tomorrow?"

"Online school. The Petersons need a pest inspection, Mrs. Blanton says there's a funny smell from the crawl space, and I have to walk two Golden Retrievers over in Crescent Cove."

"Careful there. Betsy says the whole neighborhood is crawling with those lobster-looking things," her mother said.

"Joyner demons," Maddy muttered. Joyner demons, as all the supernaturals, had been named by the kids after unpopular teachers or celebrities.

"Speaking of bites, did you know Mr. Dunkle almost got bitten by a vampire?" Mr. McDougal said as they sat in front of bowls of steaming spaghetti and dehydrated meatballs.

"How?' Maddy replied, twirling her pasta on her fork. "All I ever see them do is whine."

Traditional vampire folklore was wrong, as it happened. The would-be night crawlers existed as anemic weaklings with the mystical powers of a flowerpot. Mr. McDougal related the story as he sopped up meat sauce with a piece of garlic bread. "Apparently, one was sitting in the back seat of his car crying over a girl and –

Maddy's business phone rang. "Maddy McDougal speaking," she said crisply.

79

"Hey, can you cover my shift tonight?" LeeAnn Kingston lived down the block and usually took Thursday night patrols.

"Sure, what's up?"

"One of the Edwards keeps singing at my sister's window. I'm gonna have to stake him. Problem is, all of his whining attracted a herd- you know how their voices carry- so I have to deal with them too."

"Need some help?" Maddy asked.

"Nah, I'm good."

Maddy laid out her tactical gear. The food drops usually contained extra supplies hidden in the cans and boxes, which she stored and distributed to the others. She dressed and secured her weapons, patting her grenade pouch for good luck.

A quick sweep of the neighborhood revealed nothing out of the ordinary. As she crossed Beach Road, Maddy noticed a light on in what had been a souvenir shop. She stowed her bike in the shrubs and crept to a back window to get a peek. To her dismay, Franco sat perched on a desk while the Crester demons from the fire station shouted into a speakerphone. Maddy slid the window up so she could hear.

"... when you promised to deliver this dimension!" The female swung her tail furiously back and forth.

Maddy moved to the side of the building and hoisted herself through a half open window. She tiptoed down the hallway and stood flush against the wall while the elderly couple continued to argue with the unidentified caller, whose voice was faint, but somehow familiar.

"Be patient. The portal cannot be re opened for at least three weeks."

"We had a deal," the male demon said. "You failed to deliver this dimension unoccupied. Worse, you stuck us in Florida. *Florida*. You have twenty-four hours, then the bridges go down tomorrow at midnight. If we're stuck here, we may as well feast on the entrails of the inhabitants."

The female hit the speaker button to end the call. Franco hopped out the window and disappeared into the moonlight.

Maddy headed back to the window, accidentally kicking a discarded soda can across the floor.

"Oops."

The Crester demons pounced. In the blink of an eye, they hopped into the room and pulled her back through the window by the ankles.

"Dinner," the female cooed as Maddy hit the floor with a thud. The man wrinkled his nose.

"She's too old. And no fur. I told you we should have hit the pet shelter."

"Beggars can't be choosers," the other demon insisted, baring three rows of razor-sharp teeth.

Maddy frantically reached behind her neck for the emergency grenade pouch sewn into her jumpsuit.

"Do we have any Tabasco?" the male Crester asked.

The female continued dragging Maddy across the floor by her ankle, smacking her lips in anticipation. Maddy's fingers found the zipper to her neck pouch but it was stuck on the fabric.

"Hey, you can't eat my friend!"

Maddy twisted on the floor and gasped when she saw LeeAnn launch herself through the window holding a crossbow.

"Oh goody, dessert," said male Crester.

Maddy gave one last tug and zipper freed. She shoved her hand inside and pulled out the grenade. Yanking the pin out with her teeth, she grunted at LeeAnn, who fired steel arrows at the male. Maddy tossed the grenade down the she-demon's throat. Cresters had no esophagus so once it cleared the last row of teeth, it tumbled into her digestive tract.

"Bon appetite," Maddy said. She wriggled loose and launched herself out the window with LeeAnn just before the explosion.

"Thought you had vamps to dust," Maddy said.

"It was easier than I thought. I started singing Billie Eilish songs and they staked themselves."

"We have a problem," Maddy told her. "A big one."

Once the residents pressed the issue after weeks of being fed the sick Canadians/Super Covid story, the governor finally admitted that an unexplained, burst of dark matter had caused the rip in space at the beach. But, Maddy reasoned, if someone on this side had been working with the demons, that meant the portal opening hadn't been random. If the bridges went down while the creatures were still on the island, that would be bad for the folks on the mainland and everywhere else.

Friday morning, Maddy headed to the beach pavilion. LeeAnn, Matthew Delaney, Charlie Feldman and the Hogar twins waited.

"So you really think it's true? Someone opened up that portal on purpose?"

LeeAnn asked.

Maddy nodded. "We have to take them all out before they lower the bridge tonight at midnight."

"How?" Charlie said.

"I'm going to see a man about a cat, that's how," Maddy said. "Get everyone suited up and ready."

Maddy pedaled home and brought up her zoom app. Mr. Robinson's anxious face appeared.

"Maddy, is everything all right?" he whispered.

"Tell me about your trip to Switzerland last year. And your cat."

While taking care of Franco over the past weeks, Maddy had occasionally noticed a particular knick-knack or family picture. One photo showed the couple on a Swiss ski slope. Another photo had a blurry background of the CERN complex on the Franco-Swiss border. Mr. Robinson had a Ph.D. in particle physics and a keen interest in time travel, according to the diplomas on the office wall and the contents of his bookshelf.

Maddy leaned in closer to the monitor. "I'll start. You visited the Large Hadron Collider in Geneva, right? I read all about the Higgs Boson research going on there. And later you cut some kind of deal with Franco's pals to use it and that's what caused all this, am I right?"

Mr. Robinson went pale. "Franco's a consultant for universe hoppers.

He said we'd be able to go to any parallel dimension of our choice. My wife could be a real princess.

"What about the rest of us?"

"He said there would be a flash and everything would be gone- the natural completion of the Big Bang cycle," he whimpered. "They'd re boot the galaxy, terra form a sun and stars, divide up the planets among themselves. It would be painless and quick for everyone else."

"Call me back in an hour or I guarantee you I won't be painless or quick," Maddy snapped.

Her next stop was the vampire's lair with LeeAnn. The Edwards were none too pleased when they burst through the front door of the restaurant, letting in the glare of the mid day sun.

"Listen up losers. The world is going to end at midnight if you don't stop whining. We need you at the south bridge," Maddy announced.

One of the Edwards bared his puny teeth. It actually took a few hundred years for a vampire to grow a proper set of fangs. LeeAnn socked him in the mouth. Maddy laid out the situation.

"So do you want to wait a hundred years to grow fangs, or get back to normal tonight? Your choice. Prom season is right around the corner. I'm sure some girl would want to go with you. Some lonely, desperate, girl. Somewhere."

Grudgingly, the vampires agreed to Maddy's plan. She sped back to her house and fired up her laptop. Mr. Robinson's call came right on time.

"Give me the short version and tell me if my plan can work," Maddy ordered.

Mr. Robinson rubbed his eyes and spoke slowly.

"Every particle in the universe gains mass, which is to say, gets its very existence, by passing through the Higgs energy field that was discovered in Geneva with the Large Hadron Collider years ago. The field is everywhere so it literally affects the vacuum of empty space-time. The question is, how stable is the vacuum? If we knows the answer to that, we could predict *exactly* when the world will end."

"Get to the point."

Mr. Robinson continued, "We've known for some time that the universe is unstable and will eventually be wiped out and replaced with something else. In a few billion years, our sun will burn out, in the process expanding and destroying planets, including Earth. With a little help from my colleagues across the space time continuum, I just sped up the timetable a little."

"What went wrong?"

Mr. Robinson's face flushed. "I made an arithmetic error. The portal opened early and closed before the particle accelerator launched. My, uh, colleagues arrived expecting an unoccupied solar system and instead, well, they're trapped in Florida without their powers of flight and teleportation. We were stuck on the mainland. Dang tourists always clog up the roads."

"Are you nuts?" Maddy asked.

"I'm sorry! I've been stalling for time, trying to figure out how to re set the continuum, but ..."

After a brief discussion of where the triggers should be set, he confirmed that Maddy was on the right track. She reached over to end the call.

"Oh, Maddy, don't be too hard on Franco. He's kind of a big deal, highly sought on the time travel circuit. Some of the other creatures paid him handsomely to escape a dimension where they were being held captive by a giant squid."

The rest of the day passed in a blur of briefings and preparation. At ten, Maddy radioed the rest of the team and headed for the south bridge. Her parents recruited the able-bodied adults with Charlie while LeeAnn and the twins set up a perimeter with the Kardashian demons at the north bridge. It took some convincing, but eventually, the she-demons had seen the wisdom in making a deal to get back home, where they had the power of mind control as well as better outfits. That weren't nice about it, though.

"You're like, so basic," one of them drawled to LeeAnn.

Maddy was in position with the vamps when Franco, accompanied by a group of demons, walked toward the bridge. On her walkie, LeeAnn confirmed a group of supernaturals was approaching the north bridge at the same time.

"It's go time," Maddy whispered.

The demons took a running hop towards the bridge tender's station. When they were almost to her position she yelled, "Now!" and tossed two throwing stars in quick succession at the crab creatures. They howled in agony as the Edwards started singing "To Die For."

The Bellas shrieked, "Edward, don't leave me!"

Their voices carried all the way from one end of the island to the other, signaling the team to initiate phase two. The Edwards' song selection operated as a back up signal for each phase of the operation in case the radios got damaged or malfunctioned.

Maddy placed the modified holographic projector on the ground at the precise location Mr. Robinson had provided. Across the island, residents readied for battle. Maddy picked off the demon onslaught one at a time with her crossbow, silently counting down with the timer display on the projector. Her dad watched through binoculars from a condo roof, gleefully celebrating each blow. "Good one honey! Hit him again!"

At the north bridge, the Kardashians helped team LeeAnn by hurling rocks, staplers, insults, whatever they could find, at the horde to prevent the bridge from coming down.

"That tail is so last season," one of them taunted.

Meanwhile, the twins manned the beach, beating back the sea creatures and homicidal seagulls while tourists dueled hand to hand with the shark heads and assorted two-natureds across the island.

At 11:56 p.m., the projectors hummed. On cue, the Edwards broke into "I Won't Give Up On Us," signaling everyone to get ready to toss the supernaturals through the portal.

Maddy pointed at her feline nemesis. "Franco? Come with me if you want to live."

Hissing all the way, the tabby followed her to the foot of the bridge. Maddy removed Franco's collar, the last element, and popped open the nametag, revealing a small keypad. Maddy had deduced that Franco wasn't climbing Banyan trees for the view- he'd been trying to create an aperture so he could get back home.

"Climb," Maddy commanded.

Franco slunk toward a pepper tree and jumped to the tallest point. As soon as his paws touched the branch, the hum got louder until it could be heard on the whole island. The Edwards broke into the chorus of "Cardigan," their grand finale, and went back to moping.

A portal opened about a hundred feet above a lifeguard station and spread through the sky. Assorted supernaturals screamed as the team hurled them into the air and back home through the abyss.

The Kardashians waved goodbye. "Later, losers."

Across the island, the team herded supernaturals through the portal. Some jumped in voluntarily, reasoning that at least the giant squid provide free dental care. Others simply threw in the towel, admitting they'd underestimated the locals. When the portal squeezed shut, Mr. Robinson's devices blinked one last time and re set the timeline. The couple that had been lost during their boat escape popped back up in the Gulf. The vampires went back to staring at their phones and complaining about the cell signal.

Franco poised to jump.

"Not so fast," Maddy said. She scooped him up in her messenger bag.

"You get to stay here and be a housecat. That's the price you pay for messing with us," she whispered.

In the days that followed, Maddy and her friends received medals of valor, for helping to maintain order during the influenza "quarantine." The kids continued to gather on Thursdays for training exercises at the church parking lot, just in case. While they go through their paces, Franco watches from his perch, high in a banyan tree, plotting his revenge.

Alien Apple

Guy Belleranti

The apple in my kitchen
Looked like a yummy snack.
I picked it up, took a bite—
The apple bit me back!

"Ouch!" I yelped in pained surprise.
"Sorry," the apple cried.
"I did not want to hurt you,
But you hurt my outside!"

"You bite, you talk, and you hurt?"
I set the apple down.
"What kind of strange fruit are you?"
I asked with a big frown.

"I'm an alien apple
From a faraway place.
I took a lot of wrong turns
And became lost in space."

I found a map and pointed.
"Here's where we both are now."
"Wow!" it said. "I can get home.
"Your sky map shows me how!"

The apple gave me kisses
On neck and ears and face.
Then it soared out the window
And into outer space.

Who?

Formerly a laboratory technician-turned-home-educator, **Richard H. Fay** now spends his days creating art. He often draws inspiration from history, myth, folklore, and legend. Many of the fruits of Richard's creative labours have appeared in various e-zines, print magazines, and anthologies. Merchandise featuring Richard's artworks and designs sell internationally through several online print-on-demand stores

Norman Birnbach is a short story writer and humorist whose work has appeared in the Magazine of Fantasy & Science Fiction, McSweeney's Internet Tendency, The New York Times, The Wall St. Journal and other publications. A native New Yorker, he lives in Chilmark, MA, with his wife, three children and their dog named Taxi. Follow him on

Twitter: @NormanBirnbach or visit his website: normanbirnbach.com.

Pamela Love was born in New Jersey. After graduating from Bucknell University, she worked as a teacher and in marketing before becoming a writer. She's published more than a half-dozen books, with her latest, A Prayer and a Pickaxe, published last year by Pauline Books and Media. Dozens of her poems and stories have appeared in such magazines as Spaceports and Spidersilk, Cricket, and Page & Spine. She and her family live in Maryland.

Lawrence Buentello has published short stories in a variety of publications and greatly enjoys writing fiction for young people. He lives in San Antonio, Texas.

Thomas Vestaas is the pen name of Jørn Arnold Jensen. Jensen works as a communication advisor in the small city of Kristiansand in the southern part of Norway, and when he finds the time, he writes short stories. In 2018 he had a science fiction collection out in Norwegian, and he has published a few stories and essays, mostly in online magazines. He is currently working on a new book and is also busily engaged with his four grandchildren.

Rose Hollander lives in Massachusetts, for now. She keeps her shoes tied and her glasses straight.

Kim Bonner is a native Floridian and a graduate of Stetson University. Her work has appeared in the Flying South Literary Magazine and the Barely South Review. Writing as Kim English, her picture books are available on Kim-English.com

Lisa Timpf is a retired HR and communications professional who lives in Simcoe, Ontario. Her poetry has appeared in *Star*Line, Eye to the Telescope, New Myths, Liminality,* and *Polar Borealis*. You can find out more about Lisa and her writing projects at http://lisatimpf.blogspot.com/.

Francis Wesley Alexander is the author of *I Reckon* (Bottom Dog Press), a book of haiku and haibun; and *When the Mushrooms Come* (Alban Lake), a science fiction book of drabbles. The five-time Rhysling nominee has had haiku, haibun, and scifaiku published worldwide in *Spaceports & Spidersilk, Illumen, Space and Time*, and others.

Tony Daly is a poet and short story writer of fantasy, science fiction, horror, and military fiction. His work was recently published in Illumen, Silver Blade, The HorrorZine, and The Stray Branch. He is proud to serve as an Associate Editor with Military Experience and the Arts. For a list, that probably needs to be updated, of his published work, please visit https://aldaly13.wixsite.com/website or follow him on Twitter @aldaly18.

David C. Kopaska-Merkel assumed human form in the 50's. As a cover, he edited *Star*line* in the late '90s, and won the Rhysling award (long poem) in 2006 for "The Tin Men" (a collaboration with Kendall Evans). His poetry has been published in venues including *Asimov's*, *Strange Horizons*, *Polu Texni*, *Primate Cuisine*, & *Night Cry*. He has written 31 books, and edits *Dreams and Nightmares* magazine; @DavidKM on Twitter.

Guy Belleranti writes fiction, non-fiction, poetry, puzzles and humor for both children and adults. His children's writing has appeared in many publications including Highlights for Children, Fun For Kidz, Jack and Jill, Humpty Dumpty, and Spaceports & Spidersilk. In addition, he's had fiction, nonfiction, poetry and puzzles published by educational organizations such as ProQuest, Super Teacher Worksheets, Schoolwide and MATH Worksheets 4 Kids. Guy also has had six leveled reader books published by RR Books (aka Reading Reading Books). He worked for many years in school libraries and is a long-time docent educator at the local zoo. His author's website is www.guybelleranti.com/

CPSIA information can be obtained
at www.ICGtesting.com
Printed in the USA
BVHW042219200221
600714BV00009B/170